Chthon Press/Assembly Line Studio.

Designed, Published and Printed in the United States of America

Copyright ©2022 by Paul JJ Payack

First Edition

All Rights Reserved

For more information and interviews, call 1.737.215.7750 or email pauljjpayack@gmail.com.

The Dream Cycle:
Selected Metafictions
on Dreams and Dreaming

By Paul JJ Payack

Dedication

The Dream Cycle is dedicated to my two granddaughters:

Guadalupe "Lupita" Beatriz Roman-Payack

and

Loudres "Lola" Paz Roman-Payack

Special thanks to my wife, Millie Lorenzo Payack, who has been the first to read the tales in this book as they passed through various incarnations over the years, and my twin brother, Peter Payack, who encouraged me to resurrect an earlier version of this manuscript (circa 2004). I should also mention my daughters Rebecca (Bekka) Ashley and Elisabeth Lauren for their steadfast support of my work.

Table of Contents

Dedication 4
Nihil Obstat 9
Outcast's Assertion 10
Author's Preface 11
Idiot's Tale 15
IN PRAISE OF FALLING STARS, ... 17
Inventive Memory 18
A Tale Well Worth Repeating 19
UNSPEAKINGS OF THE UNPERSON 20
The Boiling of the Seas 21
Wringing Out Dreams 22
Midget's Tale 23
In Distrust of Memory 27
The Deep Thinker 27
Fluid Dynamics 28
The Hierophant 29
The Dreamer's Eye I 30
The Dreamer's Eye II 31
Prognosis: Death 32
Dissonance, Harmony, and Counterpoint 33
A Happy Ending 33
BARBATO ET CAUDA 34
The Bottom Line, ... 35
A Prose Sequence 35
The Fugitive 37
Xinjiang Proverb 39
I Weep Where I Once Ruled 40

The Thunderer	41
Terminus Veritatis	42
NOWHERE (Which Lies to the East of NOPLACE)	44
The Official Searcher of Hearts	45
Crystallization of the Unconscious	46
The Authorized Version of Reality	47
To Ask for Bread and Receive a Stone	48
Consciousness	49
He Began His Writing Believing …	50
To Proceed Obliquely	51
Dream-slayer	53
Short Story	54
Radix Malorum	55
A Two-line Play	55
Standard Operating Procedure	56
The Duty of the Technocrats	56
Doomsday Philosophers	57
To Sleep, etc.	58
The Dreams of the Dead	58
Mythomania	60
The Applied Metaphysician	62
The Black Terror	62
The Avoidance of Dreaming	63
A Better-informed God	64
Challenging the Delusional	64
Prologue to *Children of the Mind*	67
The Cosmic Call	68
Daring the Fearful Thing	70
THE DREAM-CHILD	73
Zanichelli's Tale	74
DREAMS TO ASHES TURNED	76

Godh is Everywhere	77
The Black Sky	77
Dream-stuff	79
Ecce Homo	80
Etched on a Clay Tablet	82
In a Cuneiform Script	82
Microtale	83
Tale Without a Hero	84
The Evocatio	85
The Face of His Father	86
First Principles	87
NHA	88
On the Nature of Metafiction	89
The Steppingstone to the Stars	90
Stone-clouds #2	92
Storming the Computers	93
Surrealist's Nightmare	94
ULČ	95
Worlds to Shatter, Shattered Worlds	97
Worlds to Shatter, Shattered Worlds	100
Dream Sequence No. 1	103
Abraham Lincoln	103
Dream Sequence No. 2	104
Aristotle	104
Dream Sequence No. 3	105
Heraclitus	105
Dream Sequence No. 4	107
Duns Scotus	107
Dream Sequence #5	108
Claude Monet	108
Dream Sequence No. 6	109

Johann Sebastian Bach	109
Dream-Vision #7	110
Dream-Vision #8	111
Retelling the Tale	111
Demosthenes	111
The Wall Builders	112
Disengaged from Reality	114
The Dream-drive	114
The Story of Ulugh Beg	115
The Tales	117
The Polymath	118
What is a Dream?	119
Weak Imagery	122
The Noers-of-Nothingness	122
Whatever is Not Forbidden	124
Selected Bibliography	125
About	139
Paul JJ Payack	139
Index	142

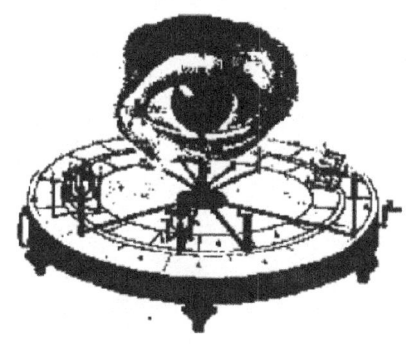

Nihil Obstat
Collage by Paul JJ Payack

Outcast's Assertion

———————— ▼ ————————

"Dreams alone can keep a man alive."

-- Paiacus

Author's Preface

▼

In the Spring of 1973 Millie and I drove from Cambridge out to neighboring Groton to visit her nursing school roommate, Michelle, her husband Steve, and three-year-old daughter, Karen.

They had agreed to run a small farm in exchange for living in an authentic New England stone farmhouse. This vision of a bucolic, romantic 'little-women-esque' country life was quickly punctured for Millie, upon learning that the day before we arrived, these latter-day Alcott's had slaughtered Karen's 350-pound pet. We are 'cat people'; we would never eat our cat. I mention all this because this was the week that one Pablo Diego Jose Francisco de Paula Juan Nepomuceno de los Remedios Cipriano de la Santisima Trinidad Ruiz y Picasso died, (April 9, 1973).

In his *New York Times* obituary published the following day, I learned of the astonishing productivity of the artist: some 100,000 creative works, with about 8,500 of which were considered 'major'. This captivated my mind for the entire weekend. Now I date my fiction writing career to May 24, 1971, when I first attempted to construct a 'tale' with all the requisite components. Thankfully, little or no evidence of this first foray have survived.

My dear friend and mentor, the author Sylvia Leah Berkman, suggested that I was endeavoring to "write a bookshelf" rather than a number of disparate, unrelated works. I took Sylvia's comments to heart.

I then took the *Times* estimate of 8,500 major creative works over some eighty years to mean that Pablo Diego Jose created about 106.25 works per year (or about two every week). Looking back over the last couple of years, I saw that I had created some fifty-three 'tales' (later to be re-Christened as 'metafiction'), or about two per month in that period. Picasso's rate of creation was some three times mine, and he sustained, and in some ways actually increased this prodigious output over six-plus decades!

By the end of this bucolic weekend, even an arrogant, young, Harvard student was forced to admit that all productivity comparisons were rendered moot. Even now looking back over some fifty years, I have authored about 700 metafictions and 400 wordless tales or collages) vs. about 100,000 creative works of which eighty-five hundred are considered major. Game, set, and match to Monsieur Picasso.

Now after half a century and hundreds of tales, poems, collage narratives, polyplays, polyphonic prose pieces, flash- and metafictions, I thought it might be interesting to take a cross-section of my work that mention dreams, visions, nightmares, prophesies, and the like and arrange them in a pseudo-random order. The resulting juxtapositions would only add to the dream-like experience of reading the collection, themselves often bits and pieces of larger works, sometimes separated by vast distances in time, geography, and psychographic history.

PJJP
Texas Hill Country
October 2022

Idiot's Tale

▼

Author's Note: From a distance of some forty years, I can no longer recall if the following was a dream, vision, memory, or admixture of all three.

An Idiot approached me the other day (previously he had spoken to me but once, "All reality is saturated with meaning," he said at that time, but I digress) and unburdened himself of the following tale which he claimed to have found fluttering about behind his eyes in the depths (the word is his) of his head:

In land where the Sun shone from the North was a man who spent his whole life in pursuit of that polygon which is all corners. Shunned as if defiled by some dread disorder, old men spat in his face as the children would flee from his shadow. A sign of the Cabal was branded upon his brow (that all men might see, and his head was half-shaven. Though considered among the lowest of men, he was never forbidden his freedom. He roamed hither and yon yet in no quarter was his crime overlooked or forgiven. And though he was never to say it (his tongue had been extricated), his hollow eyes revealed his anguish and the deepness of his remorse. It was the vilest of crimes he had committed. (It was said to have occurred in a moment of pique.) And though this would never he spoken of (the taboo was too strong) the nature of his crime was obvious to all:

He had dared the destruction
  Of a single Human thought.

In Praise of Falling Stars

———————— ▼ ————————

Three persons (one white, one purple
and one green) gathered about the great
black monolith which they had previously
ascertained had fallen from a passing star.
Their comments, (recorded for all posterity by
a disinterested passerby):
(1) 'Heresy can best be viewed as
treason against God.
(2) 'I find no shard of evidence,
either in empirical data or the
professional literature, to show
that there are factories
that manufacture our dreams,

(3) 'This presages a struggle in which
the Dreamers will stand on one
side and the Men of Vision on
the other.'

12.1 (IX) (24:18) #394

Inventive Memory

▼

& in the digging they

uncovered some

forgotten old truths and encountered

some very ancient dreams....

6.22 (19) #306

A Tale Well Worth Repeating

Melampos

———————— ▼ ————————

In olden times Melampos* walked the Earth. A prophet by trade, he was well-schooled in the language of Worms. Events conspired as they sometimes do and our friend the prophet was thrown into a dungeon for "finding Truth in a well".

While there he inadvertently overheard the worms conversing amongst themselves, the gist of their conversation was that the roof overhead was about to fall in, for the beams had been eaten through. Alarmed, Melampos called this to the attention of his captors; subsequently, he was moved to an adjacent hold in the compound and, just as he had predicted, the beams did indeed rot through.

The King, amazed and a bit terrified at the prophet's strange ability, not only released Melampos but also rewarded him with several yoke of oxen. However, from thence forward Melampos was remembered by the populace as a *A Dreamer of 'Air Castles'; also, a euphemism for fool.

6.15 (1) (26:6) #464

Unspeakings of the Unperson

(Excerpts from the Catechism

▼

Q. What is fate?
A. The residue of one's life.
Q. What is life?
A. The unfolding of consciousness.
Q. What is consciousness?
A. Consciousness can best be construed as a dreamer dreaming in an inscrutable tongue.

....
....
..................13 (IV) (45:17) #746

The Boiling of the Seas

▼

When the Procurator declared all Dreamers "born today and dead yesterday," and labelled the Imagination as a disease of the most virulent sort, the workers of land rose in spontaneous rebellion.

The Dreamers put their ears to the ground only to hear the thunderous hooves of the legions of the Procurator storming ever closer.

Eventually, the Dreamers and Thinkers were trampled into dust.

In the aftermath of a situation such as this, one of two events is certain to occur (probability of 1); all others are certain not to occur (probability of 0):

Such is the anger of the remaining populace that the seas boil, or time passes & people forget.

Wringing Out Dreams

―――――― ▼ ――――――

It was in the Land of YNCE (inch) that the equation was first derived that the life of a free man was worth that of precisely 847 born to slavery.

It was also in the land of YNCE (inch) that following curiosities were said to be found:

(1) If you compressed the dust,
you would bring out blood,

(2) If you squeezed the sand,
you would wring out dreams,

(3) If you breathed the air, it would issue forth cries.

8.26 (III) (41:3) #670

Midget's Tale

▼

While wandering about the bowels of Harvard's Widener library, I came upon a midget in one of the darker cubicles I had never seen before. I quickly ascertained that he was agitated in the worst possible way.

Thinking that I might be able to lend some assistance I went over to him and started to speak in what I thought to be a soothing tone. Noticing that that my words fell upon deaf ears, I resigned myself to watching this rather curious demonstration.

He then related the following tale to me that I am reproducing as if it were told in a logical & coherent manner.

It seems that one day, not too long ago, he acquired a highly valued stack pass (through what means I do not know). though through innuendo it was clearly nefarious),

He came upon a thin volume by a little-known author and published by an unknown house that concerned itself with the history of a people who were remembered, he told me, only for the fact that they conversed in a universal tongue called Mathano. (Though, of course, there were those who insisted 'Mathematico'; was the proper appellation.

It was the fact that the volume was missing that led to his current perturbation. Harvard supposedly possessed the only extant copy and now this, too, was missing.

Anyway.to describe the physical and psychological state of the man as disheveled would be too kind an equivocation.

The midget went on to describe the landscape of this place in great detail: it was a watery place, a single grain of sand was considered a dune three a desert; the sailing ships were composed of light; courses of action were decided upon through the observation of dust on cubes of blackness; to walk over the abyss was considered sport; volume was diminished simply through the rearrangement of mass; shadows would persist for centuries: Sawdust and broken glass were considered commodities of the most valuable sort; the stars were thought to be in one's head; the trees were planted daily in co-ordination with the colour of the sky; moon baths had the inverse effect as those of the double suns, and so on. It was here that his speech became completely incomprehensible and soon, he scurried out of my vision, and back into the stacks.

I never saw him again, not that afternoon nor any other after that. When I later related the whole story to my wife, Millie, she believed my every word (she thought the midget to be cute) but she insisted that there was some part of it that I had failed to divulge. I indicated it was true. I had hidden from her one pertinent fact: those who inhabited this land needed a license to speak certain words, another to think certain thoughts, and another still to dream even the most ordinary of dreams.

When I mentioned this point, she said she knew it would turn out like that and, when I think back on it, so did I. As a matter of fact, I recall considering the midget's tale a complete fabrication until he made known this final point, (thinking not even a madman could have invented such a tale).

Whether his story about the book was reality or fiction, I cannot rightly say. After pursuing the question, I have found no mention in any history (reputable or otherwise) of such a land and the card catalogue lists no such volume. Furthermore, the head librarian insisted

they were never in possession of such a
one, and that none had ever existed.

10.12 (9:3) #183

In Distrust of Memory

The Deep Thinker

▼

A system is constructed that is so close to perfection that dreamers are considered superfluous.

Not knowing that such a course of action is only for the gods to decide, the Dancing Madness comes to grip the populace in which grumbles quickly escalate into roars and there is much incanting at the moon.

In due course, a Deep Thinker with a highly developed word sense, attempts to order meaning out of this chaos by adding stones to the temple, and other assorted idiocies.

Needless to say, his efforts failed, and he is sent into exile during which time he chronicles the whole affair in a disquisition entitled,

'In Distrust of Memory'.

8.11 (21:9)

Fluid Dynamics

———————▼———————

Those in this place fed upon MANNA, AMBROSIA
and the MANDU of the ancient Hindus.

There they would sit quite
comfortably upon rainbows, bending each other's
eyes considering realists only
those dreamers who believed in miracles.

12.29 (XV) (15:15) #257

The Hierophant
A Text from Footnotes Culled

▼

Previously thought to be little more than an imposter magician, the Hierophant gain the respect of the priesthood and world-at-large through his construction of a new, sacred text from the footnotes of the old volumes.

His method was an original one: he employed mirror images and neologisms. The result was, the critics agreed, quite remarkable. It was a text with no beginning and no end; This was so since he employed no words. (It was a book of echoes.) Between its covers could be found Hellfire, the lives of illustrious ancestors, dreams made visible and much, much more.

The title: *The Future Belongs to those Who Dare*.

7.6 (19 :15) #315

The Dreamer's Eye I

─────── ▼ ───────

Zyblya relates that on the day that the Dreams passed thru, the Evil Endless Realm collapsed. Theologians attributed the event to an Act of God, mathematicians to the 'x' in an unknown equation, but I much prefer the mere existence of faith in a faithless age.

7.27 (X) (20:12) #327

The Dreamer's Eye II

▼

'The Baptismal Ceremony calls for each new convert to be immersed in the residue of the Dreams.

—Handbook of Ritual VIII.23.i-iii

8.19 (III) (20:13) #344

Prognosis: Death

───────── ▼ ─────────

Zencle, the physician, defined in layman's terms
his patient's hitherto unknown illness as,

'...Recurring dreams, a deteriorating

yet chronic condition with no known cure

and little chance for a recovery to normal life:

prognosis: death'.

9.3 (II) (22:2) #349

Dissonance, Harmony, and Counterpoint

or A Happy Ending

▼

Pulling and pushing the

Dreams toward the Abyss

the Evil-mongers ventured

to near the edge and they,

too, tumbled in.

3.19 (VI) (20:16) #347

Barbato Et Cauda

Bearded and Tailed

▼

Being a List of the Eight Things
Elicited by the Arrival of Comets:

1) Wind

2) Famine

3) Plague

4} Death to Kings

5) War

6) Earthquakes

7) Floods

8) Dreadful change

2.2 (VI) (24:10)

The Bottom Line,

Or a Prose Sequence

▼

The wizard ascends the mountain in his quest for TRUTH. Atop the summit he spies a massive squall; knowingly he nods his head. The ground shakes and the earth quakes; a wry smile faintly passes over his lips.

A triple thunderbolt forks over his head and from the sky falls a rain of fish; ever so slightly his eyes brighten.

Descending this same mountain, he remarks to no one in particular, *Today, I witnessed TRUTH thrice.'

(But, in truth, he had witnessed no such thing.) Later, two children enter the meadow beneath the peak (through which the wizard had just passed).

They pay witness to the whistling of an arrow, the sound of a shepherd's pipe,

the splash of water, the
hissing of a serpent and the
scuffling of feet. Arriving
home their mother asks,
'What did you see?' to which
they both replied, 'Nothing.'
(But, in TRUTH, they had
witness much.)

9.15 (13:11) #225

The Fugitive

▼

She was sought without relent. Some wished to dismember her with the strokes of a quill. Others sought to destroy her through skillful elocution. When she came into the open, they would seek to hide her; when she was hidden, they sought her out. She was considered to be radical by some, reactionary by others, and dangerous to all. The company she kept was suspect. (In the dark night, knocking on wooden doors was to be heard. Sharp words would be exchanged. And those who kept her close to heart would be carted off into the unknown.) Yet her enemies would never wholly meet with success.

(She was made of sturdier stuff.) It is true that there would be ages when her voice was seldom to be heard but there were others when she would be shouted as the thunder. (It was widely believed that children would quickly befriend her. It was, also, said that old men would cry out her name at the hour of their death.) Constant was her virtue and VERITAS is her name.
*

If this name be unfamiliar to you, weep, and pray that your children live to see a better day.

2.20 (1) (4:62) #134

Xinjiang Proverb

——————— ▼ ———————

Some men teem in their bodies;
for others the teeming is of the mind.

11.25 (I) (45:15) #692

I Weep Where I Once Ruled

───────── ▼ ─────────

It was in the Land of YNCE (inch) that the equation was first derived that the life of one free man was worth that of precisely 847 born to slavery. It was also in the land of YNCE (inch), that the following curiosities were said to be found:

(1) If you compressed the dust, you would bring out blood,

(2) If you squeezed the sand, you would wring out nightmares, and

(3) If you breathed the air, it would issue forth cries.

8.26 (III) (41:3) #670

The Thunderer

▼

He possessed that ability to fabricate phrases which would literally leap off the printed page, pass through the consciousness of the reader, and finally, lodge themselves indelibly in the memory.

More simply put it was the gift of stuffing old dreams into new heads.

9.26 (III) (37:3) #617

Terminus Veritatis

———————▼———————

With great precision did the medical team from the Center for the Struggle Against Ideological Deviation make their predetermined incisions.

The patient lay on the operating table for four hours and more. The bright lights of the operating theatre glared overhead; the life-sustaining machines whirred ceaselessly.

The smell of antiseptic hung in the air of the waiting room as the comrades of the beloved waited, staring blankly, into the drabness, their ashen faces, anxiously attempting to occupy their blank minds, wringing what little compassion remained, clutching their hands around the rapidly dissipating hope.

The surgeons stoically emerged. With great solemnity, the chief surgeon declared the operation to be a failure. The patient's body had been filled with the dreaded cancer. To their horror they had discovered that TRUTH had spread throughout his entire system. There was no hope of remission.

Every nook and cranny of the patient's body had been filled with the dreaded cancer. It was better this way for all concerned.

5.27 (I) (40:14) #659

NOWHERE (Which Lies to the East of NOPLACE).

▼

There are to be found:

--a graveyard of faded memories

--fields sown with false hope-

-and a home for lost dreams'.

The Official Searcher of Hearts

———— ▼ ————

Official Searcher of Hearts
(wearing his Crown of Immortality)
peered into his Box of Dreams and
pronounced, "On this moment hangs
eternity; repeated moments produce
experience."

"Yes,' replied the Keeper of the Imperial Archives (his old and
venerable adversary) with a great
stammering of lips, "… but only if falsehood
can also be viewed as truth".

Crystallization of the Unconscious

▼

On the day that the Last of the Last had achieved the precise manipulation of dreams thru a highly technical process known only as the 'crystallization of the unconscious'. A young (and now lost) Aristotle was one of the few to realize that the event presaged a false epistemology.

The words he inscribed in his notebooks,

'Today, even the mirrors must remain veiled.'

7.27 (VI) (20:3) #323

The Authorized Version of Reality

▼

And it was declared that

the THINKERS take it

upon themselves

to construct a New Vision

thru which all

might better see.

11.5 (1):16) #230

To Ask for Bread and Receive a Stone

▼

When the people of Naxos finally stormed the Citadel of the Infidel in order that they might regain the long-suppressed Right to Dream, they were brutally repulsed and, to the last, had their thumbs secured by screws.

The reasoning? Even the Wind Belongs to the King!

10.13 (V) (23:8)

Consciousness

———————— ▼ ————————

'Consciousness, the movement of
the mind both in recognizing its own
shape
and in maintaining that configuration
in the face of change, can also be
construed
as the Mysteries of Fate and the
power
of the gods'.

6.13 (IV) (26:4) #462

He Began His Writing Believing ...

He began his writing believing himself to be building that system of words which embody within itself the totality of existence. As the arrow of time winged its steady course, he never faltered or understood his task to be less than this. Carefully he arranged his words (noun and verb alike) in order to trace through the curvature of the Earth or the infinitude of Time.. The spin and strangeness of every quark were recorded in his words.

In the end he had detailed the outline of the Cosmos, (as were the breath of all the Living Things), the hiding places of suns, and the borning and dying of empires were all delineated within.

To Proceed Obliquely

▼

Thaab, the Dream-slayer, fabricated (on behalf of the Zealots), a system of windows *enabling him to peer into each man's mind. Now, to give an accurate and exhaustive account of his design would call for a far more perceptive mind than I possess but let me simply state that it is a well-known fact that the Four Elements combine into but two solids -- sulfur & mercury -- therefore, any desired substance can be produced by carefully combining these in the correct proportions. Thaab's Why and Wherefore: (Here given in a rough translation from his talismanic.)

> *All were recorded within, and when this had been done (when not an Iota or Space not Tittle of Time had escaped his quill) it was then that he understood the*

meaning hidden in the words.

"Whoso meddles in affairs that are no business of his, will hear truths that will not please him."

Dream-slayer

———————— ▼ ————————

A person suspicious by nature (see "Slayer of Dreams").

3.29 (III) (25:7) #431

Short Story

▼

It is the middle of the night. A gray-haired, wrinkled, little women, her hand shaking, gropes for the receiver in the dark. As she lifts it, a heavy voice gives her a quick start, 'Secret Police, may we help you?' She wishes to disengage the line, but duty presses her on; the words are hard but still they come:

"I wish to report a dream."

3.9 (11.12)

Radix Malorum

A Two-line Play

▼

(Words not to be engraved in stone yet, but nevertheless, deserving to be preserved.)

The Usurper:
"Are those your Dreams?

Ethleback:
'No, the Ashes of my Dreams!

Exeunt

2.5 (III) (30:3) #521

Standard Operating Procedure

The Duty of the Technocrats

▼

It was the duty of the Technocrats to introduce new dreams into the mainstream of the ancient society. Following the standard operating procedure, they programmed their thinking machines for the task, setting the controls for TRUTH. What resulted were extrapolations of the wildest sort concerning, among other things: magnetic bottles, phase transitions &, finally, the multi-dimensional non-dimension. While researching this little tale I was sorting through the various manuscripts attempting to find a single line that would best sum up my feelings to all this idiocy. There were none to be found, however, a stranger approached me and handed me a piece of paper on which were scribbled the following words: "God Himself is shamed."

Doomsday Philosophers

▼

A people without answers set about to enlarge the boundaries of human potential and ended up constructing for themselves a fools' paradise.

Working on a false assumption they banished all dreams to the zinc mines and imagination to a separate nation. I could spend much needless verbiage chronicling the further results of this fruitless experiment but let me end in stating that the whole affair has come down to us, simply as a novelty for Doomsday Philosophers.

\ To Sleep, etc.

The Dreams of the Dead

▼

Since it was thought that they might lose their minds if they were subjected to the rigors of studying Euclid, the young girls of The Society were assigned the task of keeping. alive the dreams of dead geniuses. It was a consuming yet thankless task, for they toiled for a society most kindly described as asymmetrical. However, they took their tasks quite seriously as can be seen from the motto woven into the insignia which they wore over their hearts:

TO SLEEP IS TO LET
THEM DIE.

12.19 (V) (15:5) #246

Mythomania
Dementia Mythos

———— ▼ ————

Gwalstoe, as he called himself, was the first certified case of dementia mythos (Mythomania in layman's terms) since the days of the pre-Socratic Greeks Considered dangerous by the authorities he was compelled to register his mind as a weapon. Brought to those of the medical profession who were considered to be the best in their field, the only responses they could elicit from the fellow were such statements as:
YOU WILL DIE BUT THE SONGS ABOUT YOU WILL LIVE ON FOREVER and MUCH OF THE CONFUSION OF LIFE IS STILLED WHEN YOU REALIZE THAT YOU ARE YOUR FATHER, and the like. The treatment proceeded in this manner until he was deemed incurable and, as a menace to society, the next step was incarceration. He was placed in the deepest & darkest pit available for

solitary confinement yet still his myths poured forth.
(No attempt proved effective at stopping the dreadful flow. The guards had to be specially outfitted with waxen ear plugs that their sanity might be preserved, all the townspeople in the vicinity were evacuated to emergency shelters in church basements and school auditoriums, and the surrounding countryside were declared disaster areas.)

Realizing the futility of this all (and cognizant of the bad press they were receiving), the authorities released Gwalstoe, now old and emaciated, on the proviso that he spends his remaining days wandering in the desert and other barren areas of the Earth.

Now, all this happened long, long ago or many years henceforward (I forget exactly which) but let me tell you that even today if you listen ever so closely to those sand-filled winds that now and again blow from the South, you can sometimes hear Gwalstoe's faint voice crying,

"I AM THE SOUND OF THOSE SONGS
NEVER SUNG."

The Applied Metaphysician

The Black Terror

▼

A man adept at Applied Metaphysics develops a philosophical system based on the interactions of motes of dust and drops of dew. He later comes to the conclusion that history can best be considered, at best, a cumulative art and, at worst, a meta-physical pretense consisting of one measure of logic mixed with two of absurdity. After what has come to be known as the Black Terror had enveloped the Earth, when all humanity could best be described as living half in shadows and half in shade, this dreamer of dreams, this man, this Applied Metaphysician, this thinker of thoughts and doer of deeds, arrives at the appointed hour of his death. At that moment when wolves are known to attempt to devour the sun, and logical meditation is nothing more than a heretical witticism (or grammatical fiction), these words were heard to pass over his lips:

"What is the weight of a nightmare?"

The Avoidance of Dreaming

▼

Then, one day, the Facilitators of that time constructed an Automatonnamed the Hollowed Moon out of wire, glass, various nonferrous metals and cunningly sculpted space. This was created with no program but, instead, was instilled with their own peculiar sense of logic.

At first widely hailed as an achievement of the highest rank, the mere fact of its existence was later deleted from the public records after it had demonstrated a frightening propensity for perpetrating, upon random individuals, unbearable acts resulting in excruciating pain, delirium, blindness, & death.

3.29 (II:25) #430

A Better-informed God

Challenging the Delusional

▼

Wyclif, a dim-witted monk with an infinitesimal (a quantity less than any assignable value) amount of intelligence, had worked too long in the medieval scriptorium, copying words he scarcely understood with a stylus upon dusty, old scrolls when he announced, one afternoon, to his astonished brethren that he had found out (on the authority of a middle-level Celestial official) that the world really was created by God as a joke. His brethren, drawing a conclusion from the premise, decide if this were so, Wyclif would, indeed, be the one to be the call of His trumpet. Immediately, they follow his every wish as a command.

However, soon a visitor comes upon the monetary with the news of a better-informed God. Then and there, Wyclif is run off into the streets, put into stocks and cabbages are thrown at him.

(The reason for this incomprehensible behaviour can be put quite simply: when a fixed delusion is challenged, the delusional are apt to resort to violence.

3.9 (17:6)

Prologue to *Children of the Mind*

▼

The Children of the Mind construct a cross
of seven flowers.
By day the flowers are removed by the authorities.
By night they are replaced by seven drops of blood.
These are removed and replaced
by seven wailings of the wind.
These are removed and replaced
by seven extirpated eyes.
These are removed and replaced
by seven auditory impressions.
These are removed and replaced
by seven intonations of the unconscious.
These are removed and replaced
by seven mirrors of the other.
These are removed and replaced
by seven swallowings of the sky.
These are removed and replaced
by seven breathings of a baby.
These are removed and replaced
by seven minds of the children.
These are removed and replaced
By seven Children of the Mind.

The Cosmic Call
An Unpublished Work

The play, itself, closed even before it opened. The problem was that no actor could be found to handle the assignment. Though billed as a one-act play; it consisted of, in fact, a single word.

The script read:

ENTER

The Player. Cosmic Call *

EXEUNT

Though scores auditioned for the part no one could be found who could get it exactly right.

*Stage Direction: The 'Call' should encompass that sound that the primeval super atom yawned at the instant the universe began to expand; God is but a whispered ululation of it; it.is the birth pangs of every mother and every birth; the sound of death; hope; striving; dreams aborning & dying, failure; the noise of love; the sound of a Black Hole sucking in a new-born star; a dandelion crying; **; a cat purring; shadows singing; stars imploding; rocks breathing; the blind seeing their first sight & the deaf hearing their first sounds; the sound of thinking; smoke striving; rainbows humming; computers whirring, and the like.

**Editor: word is missing from original manuscript.

Daring the Fearful Thing
Adapted from Euripides'
Iphigenia in Aulis, Line 303

Xoa himself, in his longwinded manner, made the announcement that those captives taken in the victory of the Tower over the Endless Mountains who could quote facts, in either poetry or prose, which he found interesting would immediately be released.

Every last man shivered in his boots for these were common foot soldiers of the dullest sort, excepting Myllye.

Here was a strange one, this Myllye, who called himself 'a professional dreamer by trade'. And so as one man after the other stepped forward Myllye would whisper into his ear another saving whisper. Xoa espied this strange man but allowed him to continue thinking this to be a curious modification of the idea that you didn't have to die if you could find somebody to die in your place. One after another Myllye hurled these fated ideas at Xoa with their sole denominator being the more absurd it was, the easier it was for him to believe it:

- 'energy can be derived from a solid-state device which strongly resembles earthly kitchenware'
- 'the heroic are those who die in struggles settled only by their being forgotten'
- 'the difference between idiots, morons, and imbeciles is the equivalent to a discretely shifting decimal point'
- 'lightning can be stored in a bottle much easier than thunder in a pocket'
- 'the Universe is a plasma (with a few minor exceptions like you and me scattered across it),'

The strange litany proceeded. Xoa, as if transfixed, listened to them all. Tens, hundreds, thousands of men were granted their freedom. And when at last but Myllye remained, Xoa exposed his heart to the Moon that this might change his luck.

'Speak your piece, Dreamer,' he demanded. Without hesitation Myllye pronounced, ' The only things new are those which have already been forgotten.'

'That I knew,' Xoa exclaimed.

'My mistake, ' the Dreamer replied.

His punishment was banishment to the salt mines, where he was to spend all the days of his life. However, Xoa possessed one future plan to secret a deadly potion into the Dreamer's morning gruel.

But Myllye (fully cognizant of his further fate), escaped after making himself immune by taking small and gradually increasing doses of the poison.

THE DREAM-CHILD
Before the Magnetic Monopole

▼

In the dark age before the magnetic monopole made its presence felt in the heavens there was a child who dreamt the first dreams. He did not know what to make of these awesome visions, so he let them run wild.

In later years they came to populate the Earth (for the dreams became the tribes and the tribes became the nations).

9.10 (13:9)

Zanichelli's Tale
Dreamium

Zanichelli, much to his own surprise, discovered the new element DREAMIUM under the workbench in his garage.

The only problem was that no spot on the periodic table could be found for it. Accordingly, an entirely new one (the now-famed Dream-table) was constructed.

And it was then that it came to the public's attention that the search for a whole new set of elements had barely begun. Before long it seemed as if every man, woman & child on the planet joined the hunt (the quick success of the ensuing search can be laid directly to this fact).

And the new elements would seem to appear in the most ordinary of places: TRUTHIUM in a shoebox, DREAMIUM under a mushroom, PAXIUM in a baby's crib, and MYTHIUM in the web of a spider.

Why these elements failed to surface until the time of Zanichelli's discovery is a question that has never scientifically been resolved.

The popular mind, however, has no such qualms. Zanichelli, it reasons, simply caught luck by the hair.

4.1 (IV) (18:4) #284

DREAMS TO ASHES TURNED
Briars and Thorns

A man possessing a name both unheard & unspoken, born under an evil star who expostulated a 'neural* model of reality introduced the procedure of branding BELIEVER and HEATHEN into the foreheads of the populace that the two might be distinguished. (In childhood he had survived the raiders of the barbarian hordes by subsisting upon briars and thorns in the desert.) When, some years later, he set his gaze upon the results of his indiscretions he was transformed into a blithering fool babbling, "What hath God Wrought?"

4.21 (III) (25:

Godh is Everywhere

The Black Sky
(Excerpted from *The Land of Orth*)

In a synagogue in Nineveh, on a day when the sun failed to rise and the sky turned black, Godh (not to be confused with God) came to one of the faithful in a vision, tells him that today is the day that he is to die and conveys to him the appointed hour. He conveyed this to the rabbi who, after conferring with another rabbi (and then the wind), advised him that there was nothing to be done other than for him to prepare to meet his maker.

Somehow, though, he knew his death now to be inevitable, he decided to flee from it. He borrowed a horse from the synagogue and galloped off to Jaffa. At the arrival of the appointed hour the man dropped to his knees, bowed his head & cowering awaited his fate in the middle of a non-descript street in this strange city. Three hours proceeded to crawl by, when a local townsman passed and noticed his curious condition. The first thing the faithful man did was to enquire as to the hour.

When he learned of it, he told the passerby that this was not possible, related to him about his intended fate, and how, miraculously, it seems to have passed him by. "But how could this be?" he said aloud, "Godh is everywhere' The passerby sternly intoned, "Not this Godh".
"Then it was a good thing I came to Jaffa," the traveler replied."

10.2 (9:7) #161

Dream-stuff
The Land of Zelotyp

▼

A material that only becomes
stronger as you hammer it.

9.26 (XI) (37:11) #625

Ecce Homo
The Great Man

▼

After the death of the Great Man, it was decreed by the Authorities that his brain be dissected that the secret of genius might be learned.

With the utmost skill was the grey matter lifted from his skull. Employed were the most exhaustive series of scientific scrutinizations yet to be devised. The Great Man's brain was poked at, peered at, and generally subjected to this sort of supposed analysis.

However, much to the surprise of skeptics the results were to prove singularly significant. Here I quote from the Official Results of the Experimenters — approved, of course, by the Department of the Struggle Against Ideological Deviation:

> *The Great Man's brain was found to consist of a most curious array of logic gates, null processes, alphanumeric algorithms, noise words, memory holes, number crunchers, matrices, meta-languages, incremental indices, time-slicing truncations, truth tables, & the like.cirs There*

*were also the slightest traces of
a hitherto unknown alloy
seemingly consisting of a fusion
between dream-stuff and steel.*

[Editor's Note: Might I remind the doubters among you that all that is here transcribed is in strict accordance with the facts.]

Etched on a Clay Tablet

In a Cuneiform Script

When they came for the Believers,
I professed non-Belief;
When they seized the Righteous,
I was unjust;
When they shackled the Saints,
I was a sinner;
When they murdered the dreamers,
I went sleepless;
When they disfigured the icons,
I grabbed my hammer;
When they stifled all thoughts,
I went mindless,
When they condemned all truths,
I espoused Falsehood;
When they elevated hate,
I went loveless;
When they spoke of life,
I knew only death.

Microtale
Too Deep to Operate

▼

The anti-mirage drugs did not take hold and so the operation called for was to be the standard one. However, this, too, proved to be unsuccessful for, as it was recorded in the log of the Secret Police, *'the dreams were lodged in the imagination where it was deemed that it was too deep to operate.'*

12.19 (XI) (I2:11) #253

Tale Without a Hero

▼

The Official of Hearts (Wearing his Crown of Immortality) peered into his box of dreams and pronounced, 'On this moment hangs eternity; repeated moments produce experience.'

'Yes,' replied the Keeper of the Imperial Archives, (his old and venerable adversary) with a great stammering of lips, 'but, at times, addition can best be viewed as subtraction.'

The Evocatio

▼

We, the Legions Rome, declare this city under siege. Greater honors and fuller rites are offered by Senātus Populusque Rōmānus to the deities residing within. Heed this summoning. The fall is foredoomed; you are hereby forewarned.

Upon hearing this call, Hercules abandoned the fabled city of Alexandria, deserting Anthony, and fleeing to the camp of the besieger, Octavius Caesar.

Far across the Mediterranean, a child of a race neither human nor divine clutched at his mother in its sleep. "Mother I have dreamed," he pronounced in words no man would ever chance to hear. "Lie still, my son; it is nothing," the mother softly Intoned, again in that strange tongue. The boy drifted off to sleep but, for her, such was not the case; she, too, had dreamed.

The Face of His Father
An Oft-told Tale

▼

A dream commands a young and arrogant man to seek his fate in a far-distant land. He departs at once, yet it takes many years for him to reach his destination. (Many, varied & horrid were the tales he would, one day, tell.)

When he finally arrives, he happens to glance into the cool waters of a shallow well. There he perceives not his reflection but the face of his father.

Only then does he realize his loss and his folly, for what he had journeyed so long to find was what he had long-ago left behind.

First Principles

▼

They awoke, one day, to find that they had mined out the last of the Dreams. But these they withheld from the populace to stimulate an artificial price rise (for the workings of the marketplace are always fair}.

6.28 (19:8) #308

NHA

The Purpose of the Product

▼

Nha had earlier developed the concept of 'the standardization of ideas and the interchangeability of all human thought'. He did this that he might stamp out cogitations in the same manner of God squeezing photons out of the nothingness.

His latest invention was meant to be ingested by the populace. Liquid in form, the concoction consisted of one-part dream, and two parts memory.

The purpose of the product: to help Humankind.

The intended result: to erase History.

On the Nature of Metafiction

A Short Excerpt from the

Introduction to Mythomania

by Sylvia L. Berkman

▼

"An increasing concentration of focus is achieved. The tales become shorter, often reduced to a single modest paragraph, at times even to an epigrammatic sentence or two. Verifiable historical reference dwindles and disappears. Time and place are still remote, but the locations now partake of a dreamlike antiquity, an imagined region peopled (if at all), by imaginary figures.

Characters are merely indicated in the abstract: 'an idiot,' 'the man,' 'he,' this certain gnostic,' 'the future King.' The result is to poise the tale in the everlasting, so to speak, shorn as it is of all human specificity."

The Steppingstone to the Stars
How the Zero Was Discovered

▼

In the backwaters of time, before Hammurabi compiled his Code or Akhenaton renounced the Ruling Lord of Thebes, in a region known for its heat and abundance of humankind, a man whose name perhaps will never be pronounced was working hard and long upon a treatise that had come to him from Mesopotamia.

The man was weary from long hours of concentration. The curious numeration of the Sumerians, cuneiform in construction, was uncommonly hard to decipher; it had taken its toll. He put down his dust board and repaired to the shade of a mustard tree for a short nap. Sleep came grudgingly; this was not unusual for an old man. Yet it was during this fitful sleep that he dreamt a dream.

In this dream he saw what no man had seen before. It appeared to him as the Eye of God. And this was possessed of a voice, in that it spoke to him:

> "I am Nothingness. I can be united to something and only that something remains. I can be taken away in like manner. I am Void, yet, if something is multiplied or divided by Myself, only I shall remain. In time, learned men will come to say that the Earth, itself, revolves upon Me. I am Emptiness. I will be worshipped as a secret symbol. My name will be whispered and uttered only

in select company and darkened rooms.
I am Nothing, it is true, but I am also the
steppingstone to the stars and the key
to the secrets of the atom. I shall be
called an Integer and described as Real.
I am Rational. And, most importantly, I
am Good."

Upon awakening, the unknown Hindu set down his dust board and drew upon it the Eye of God.

Thus did the Zero intrude itself upon the Universe.

Stone-clouds #2
A Yellow Icarus

———————— ▼ ————————

A Yellow Icarus (with a power derived from the dust of departed dragons and his own strength of will) travels from the land of the Glass Mountains to that area beyond the Sun where star-formation is going on and comes back with this truth, "I am returning to my fatherland for much the same reasons that I left it."

12 .4 (10:10) #180

Storming the Computers

―――――― ▼ ――――――

When the machines ruled the ancient dreams to be modern nightmares, the peasants stormed the computers. The king who would not smile, who introduced the infernal contraptions, avoided disaster by escaping into the hollowed-out earth. (Beneath a thin crust the planet was hollow & inside revolved three suns).

Many years later, the King was allowed to walk upon the surface when he agreed to conduct a study of the nuances, cadence and modifications of contrasting vowel sounds and, henceforward to substitute the word SLAVE for his name.

1-2.8 (16:5) #268

Surrealist's Nightmare
The Land of Zelotypua

———— ▼ ————

Those in the land of Zelotypua knew neither vision nor dream.

This being so, they first withered, and then they died.

ULČ

Unlearning the Epistemology

▼

After ULČ was lured by the Dreams into

the Land of the Antonyms, he spent all his time unlearning his old epistemology in order that he might embark upon a whole new way of knowing and thus eventually effect his escape from his dread captors.

The plot thickens when ULČ wins their

confidence and somehow convinces them that it would be to their nefarious benefit if they stored their immense knowledge of depravity (which, I should mention, they had long since refined into an artform), into a computer of his own design. Snared by the bait of their own hatefulness and believing that the machine will allow them the methods of developing newer and even more sinister forms of torture. They acquiesce, though reluctantly so.
However, it is only a matter of time before they find out the fact that proved the be the immediate cause of

ULČ's undoing: the computer had no

memory ….

5 .9 (1) (18:8) #288

Worlds to Shatter, Shattered Worlds
A Selection from Episode Two

―――――― ▼ ――――――

The One	(Slowly. In deep reflection. Attempting to decipher, decode, or simply recollect the dream.)

Last night I had a dream. In the dream I had wandered into a citadel. It was not quite a city of the dead, but neither was it a city of the living. The inhabitants could, perhaps, best be described as unborn tomorrow and dead yesterday.

The Other	I see.

The One	The walls of the citadel were plastered with the Unspeakings of the Unperson. What these concerned, I do not recall, however, I distinctly remember the words, WE US THEY THEM, though I cannot be sure as to their meaning.

The Other	Do proceed.

The One	I believe they were taken from what could best be described as either a catechism or sacred text known as the COSMOLOGIA. The focal point of the Citadel, apparently the purpose of the Citadel's existence was something

	called the Thousand Infinities, though no one seemed to know what these were or where they could be found. I thought this to be curious in the extreme.
The Other	Indeed.
The One	Everywhere, at all times, were crowds of people chanting. Chanting incantations. Chanting indecipherable gibberish. I could make out, however, that the imagination was considered to be a loathsome disease. I wandered about stealthily until I found myself descending a stairway leading into a dank, dark, musty cellar. In the cellar was a small wooden box. I was drawn to it out of curiosity. I lifted the lid and what do you suppose I had inadvertently stumbled upon?
The Other	The Thousand Infinities.
The One	The Thousand Infinities? This was not to be. There were no Thousand Infinities. Neither a Hundred, nor Ten, nor a Single Infinity, for that matter. I found myself running from the cellar screaming. What I was screaming I cannot exactly recall, but I have strong suspicions it concerned We and Us and They and Them. (Pausing. He is

	out of breath. He is spent.) What do you suppose it all means?
The Other	(Displaying deep disappointment.) I was hoping you'd tell me.
The One	(Shrugging, as if resigned.) I have no idea.
The Other	Then I'd say it means nothing.
The One	Nothing?
The Other	Nada. Naught. Null. Nothing. No thing.

Worlds to Shatter, Shattered Worlds
A Selection from Episode Seven

▼

The One	In my dream I dreamt I was dreaming a dream. In this dream (the dream in which I was dreaming that I was dreaming, that is) I was entrapped in a city ...
The Other	The Citadel?
The One	A city, a nameless city, a city itself besieged by dreams. (The city stood where the sun meets the sands.) (He gestures in a yonder fashion.) Fearing that an outbreak of peace was about to engulf the planet, these Evil-mongers disguised in every variety and form of ugliness. When the meeting was about to convene a thousand Black Butterflies flew into the chambers in the usual warning that an attack had been launched by the bitterest enemies of the Evil-mongers -- the Dreamers.
The Other	Of course; the Dreamers. It is only fitting.

The One	Attacking in the classical and time-honored manner, the Evil-mongers encircled the enemy city and dreamt their dreams.
The Other	I now see where this is heading.
The One	The first attack was bitterly repulsed as the Evil-mongers thought their ugliest thoughts, and so was the second. Many a beautiful dream was to die that day so fierce was the struggle. A stalemate ensued with neither side gaining the upper hand until a child was found who had already forgotten more than most had learned in a lifetime. He unleashed a mighty mirage that tipped the scales in the dreamers' favour. And so were the Evil-mongers forced to flee in rout. At this point I awoke. What do you make of it?
The Other	Hyper ... ineffable ....
The One	Meaning?
The Other	Nothing, of course.
The One	I see.
The Other	No, you don't.

The One	Some see more with their eyes closed than others see with their eyes open.
	(Unseen by the One and the Other, DHGHOMYO has approached them from stage right. The Other pays him little heed; the One is startled in a start of recognition.)
DHGHOMYO	Gentlemen. (To the One.) Why do you stare?
The One	My dream!
DHGHOMYO	So you are the one!
The One	The one?
DHGHOMYO	The one who has stolen my dream.
The Other	Your dream?
DHGHOMYO	The War of the Butterfly. I should introduce myself. I am called DHGHOMYO, a dreamer by trade.

Dream Sequence No. 1
Abraham Lincoln
A.D. 1809—1865

▼

In this dream Lincoln appears as a young boy. I interrupt his childhood game; he stands by a small pond. He looks directly into my eyes.

Already at seven or eight, he carries within himself a profound weariness. This much is obvious.

His eyes are hollow, sunken. His manner, distant, distracted. No childish things spoken of here.

Awaiting his fate, he already carries his future burden, hidden only to himself.

4.24 - 4.29.93, Paris

5.9.95, San Francisco

9.18.95, From the Prairie to the Piedmont

Dream Sequence No. 2
Aristotle
384–322 B.C.

In this dream Aristotle lies stricken, felled by the thought that many of his words, and works, will not survive his time, later times, or Time*

(The Author requests the Reader's patience, for here I translate from the Greek in a literal fashion.)

Aristotle cries out, "For it to be for them never to be, never to have been, never to, even, had have been!"

He then descends into in an untranslatable gibberish, almost a wail, a wailing of the most indescribable sort.

*Editor's Note: Ancient texts list 137 titles of works by Aristotle that, apparently, did not survive Antiquity.

5.11.95, Over the High Sierra to the Black Hills
6.21.95, Summer Solstice over the High Plains
9.18.95, From the Prairie to the Piedmont

Dream Sequence No. 3

Heraclitus

- **Flourished circa 500 B.C.**

▼

In this dream Heraclitus is standing upon or, rather, lying astride (truth be told, I do not remember which), an ancient, and dry, riverbed. The scene is not unlike those you might stumble upon in the high desert country of the American Southwest.

He looks me directly in the eyes and begins as if amidst a lecture:

"In fact, you can step in the same river twice, thrice, or even more so, provided the following three conditions are satisfied:

1. Shards of hope must be held in acute opposition to, and in distinction from, shreds of hope.

2. All relevant data must be obscured, obfuscated, or otherwise obliterated, and

3. The universal need for convergence must be tempered through the acknowledgement and acceptance of rounding errors.

9.18.95, From the Prairie to the Piedmont

9.19.95, From the Piedmont to the Prairie

Dream Sequence No. 4

Duns Scotus
A.D. 1265 – 1308

▼

In this dream Duns Scotus, The Subtle Doctor, the author of the First Principle, and the Copernicus, the Isaac Newton, Madame Curie, the Albert Einstein of his day, is lecturing upon his favorite subject: the nature of infinity and the nurturing of the infinite. He begins his discourse as per usual. "How many angelic beings can alight on the head of a pin?" There is no laughter here, only the stunned silence of respect bordering on reverence.

This towering intellect then turns toward me and, as if fully cognizant of a future that would evermore mock said discourse, smiles a knowing smile. The Good Doctor then turns his attention back to his class. *

* The headdress indicative of his Scholastic stature has come down through history as a symbol for fools: the Dunce Cap.)

Dream Sequence #5

Claude Monet

▼

In this dream Monet appears as an
old man on the grounds of his estate
in Giverny. The subject is water
lilies. Looks up from his easel and
stares distantly into the
her, peering into or, rather, gazing
upon that which only
can, would, or could, see.
- whispers, almost as if a silent sigh
or quiet cry, "I would
have painted the entire world, if
only I had a canvas large
enough",

8.29.95, 8.30.95, Over the Great Basin
9.18.95, From the Prairie to the Piedmont
9.19.95, From the Piedmont to the Prairie

Dream Sequence No. 6
Johann Sebastian Bach

A.D. 1685 - 1750

In this dream I am present in a great hall, I am standing directly in front of Johann Sebastian Bach, who is scribbling furiously. Apparently, Bach is in the midst of a creative frenzy.

Every now and again he turns to the nearby organ and plays a bit, a wisp, even a whispering of a piece that I recognize as embodying, perhaps, the basic elements of the Magnificat in D Major. He continues in the described manner for quite some time.

Eventually he takes notice of my presence; he glares at me with contempt. "If you must know," he answers in answer to my unasked question, "I do not hear the music so much as I see the music. I do not hear the notes so much as I see the notes. I do not hear the sound so much as I see the sound. I then imply record that which I have seen."

Dream-Vision #7
Tale of the Tittle

▼

Hitler appears to him in a dream-vision. He speaks no words, but it is understood that only one question is to be allowed. "What would have made difference?" he asks Der Fuhrer. "If I had learned the distinction between a jot and a tittle." he answered.

Editor's Note: A possible explanation for this strange response could be the following: *Jot* is for *Jod.* the smallest letter in the Hebrew alphabet. Tittle is the little bend or point that serves to distinguish certain letters of similar appearance. Jewish tradition mentions the letter *Jod* as being irremovable, adding that, if all the men in the world would endeavor to abolish the least letter in the law, they would not succeed. The guilt of changing these little hooks is declared to be so fierce that if such a thing were done, the world would be destroyed.nvhvtgnvvv

Dream-Vision #8

Retelling the Tale

Demosthenes

▼

As the tale is retold it changes in the retelling:

In a dream-vision the re-telling asks of Demosthenes the same question as the former yet, this time, the answer differs (however slightly):

"No, the fact of my genius did not spring from the placement of the pebbles in my mouth, rather, it arose the placement of the pebbles in my mind."

The Wall Builders
Without Exception

———————— ————————

*Even a gentle rain can be a
blow against the Empire
--Paiacus*

Walls are built for a multitude of purposes (but primarily for the purpose of walling things in or walling things out). The emperor Hadrian (AD 117-138) was a wall-builder. In history his place as a builder of walls is middling.

Hadrian's Wall cannot be compared, in stature, intent or extent, with (for example) the Great Wall whose construction was begun in the early Ch'in period.

Shih Huang Ti, who ordered that phantastic wall built, also ordered all the books antedating him burned; the people of the Middle Kingdom have a history of some three millennia when he ordered that History begin with himself. His wall ran, and for the most part still runs, some four or five hundred leagues along the historical frontier of the Middle Kingdom, the Mongolian Plateau. (Its purpose was to guard against the wild tribes of the West.)

Hadrian's Wall ran a mere seventy-three miles across the narrowest portion of the British Isles from the River Tyne to the Solway Firth. His was not a nightmare of a wall but merely a dream, measuring some eight feet of thickness and some six of height. It is said that Hadrian personally surveyed the line that was to establish the northern frontier of the Roman Empire. (Its purpose was to ward off the wild tribes of the North.)

There is something to a wall; the secret meaning of the thing. In all the history of walls it is that which never merits mention. Perhaps it should be for those who will, one day, be numbered among the wall-builders: where there are walls there are doors, without exception.

Disengaged from Reality

The Dream-drive

▼

When the Dream-drive was finally constructed, it was assumed that all the miseries of humankind would be held permanently in abeyance since the dreams would be coming to populate all the land.

However, such was not the case for the Dream-drive apparently malfunctioned and spewed forth such spontaneously generated, unmitigated catastrophes as the ENDLESS WAR, a formula altering the normal aberration of light, and an obscure form of societal amnesia in which no one could quite recall how to disengage the Dream-drive from reality.

8.26 (IV) (41:4)

The Story of Ulugh Beg
(Excerpt from *Children of the Mind*)

An interpreter of dreams in a dreamless world, the old man was among the first the Unperson had known to be nebulized. Ulugh Beg by name, he claimed a fish had revealed to him a secret, a secret that would set the clouds and sky afire. There was little question that he would be nebulized. It was only a matter of timing.

The Unperson still kept an oblique object Ulugh had presented to him as a child, in the days before parallel thinking, before people had become afraid of their own minds. That object would now be considered 'non-parallel' or 'oblique' .

Numbering an oblique artifactt among one's possessions was to be considered at best, indiscreet. Having an object once possessed by one of the nebulized was a particular indiscretion. The Unperson was anything if not discreet. Nevertheless, he kept the oblique object hidden away upstairs in a drawer. The object seemed to exert an undue influence over the Unperson, he could never quite rid it from the deeper recesses of his consciousness, such as it was.

The Tales

(Excerpt from Children of the Mind)

▼

What *The Chronicles* did not relate were 'The Tales'.

'The Tales' passed down from generation to generation. The tales concerning thought-catchers and dream-latchers and the days of uncertainty and fear: the last days of the past and the first of the future. The establishment of an elaborate all-pervasive apparatus of terror. The rise of Mildtryth, a simple, some say, fated man. The children taking to the streets shouting, "We Want Dreams" and "Give Us Back Our Minds".

So state 'The Tales'

The Polymath
Dreams as Complex Matrices of Amino Acids

▼

A Polymath who believes that dreams are nothing more than complex matrices of amino acids, becomes involved in their synthesis.

After much hesitation and many false starts (employing old concepts and new realities), he achieves his quintessential creation:

A LESSER GOD

The image originally occupying a finite space, perhaps the size of a grain of sand, begins to expand indefinitely until it finally encompasses and supplants (or becomes one with) the Polymath's corner of the world.

What is a Dream?

An Excerpt from

Worlds to Shatter, Shattered Worlds

The One   (Waving the Other aside.) Tell me then, what is a dream?

DHGHOMYO   A thing both existent and non-existent. A thing existing neither io quantity nor spatial continuity, existing perhaps, only in the mind of God. (And this God cannot be quantified.) You might even view dreams as a dihedral angle.

The Other   A dihedral angle!? I would prefer a book that makes men mad.

The One   Or a vector process?

DHGHOMYO   Rather, an undistributed middle.

The One   (Excitedly.) A minor amusement of the gods?

The Other	A contradiction in terms; the unreality principle.
The One	An unfolding story; a traveler's tale.
DHGHOMYO	The judgement of God.
	Oblique obfuscations.
DHGHOMYO	The object of knowledge.
The One	A language independent of abstract entities; the primary function of understanding, expirations, intuitions.
DHGHOMYO	(With a knowing nod.) Innate knowledge; The Secret of Time; the tomb of the muses.
The One	The subjunctive mood; the ablative case?
DHGHOMYO	A rising tide.
The Other	(Disparagingly.) The null set.
The One	(Ignoring the Other.) The whistle of `an arrow! The law of independent trials. (This bewilders even himself.) The state of the art; the coin of the realm.
DHGHOMYO	The drifting of the mind.

Weak Imagery
The Noers-of-Nothingness

In the in the years to come the Noers-of-Nothingness, too, vanished from the Earth. They were followed by those who knew the difference between doubtful visions and vision of truth, and these were followed by the Creators of the Synthetic Infinity. There came a time when the Creators warred against the Small Tribe in order to suppress their belief in the continuing evolution of the laws of physics. The Tribesmen were mercilessly slaughtered. When only a handful of them remained, they were herded into a clearing where the following exchange took place.

'Recant or you shall die!'

'Never, as long as we possess a single breath."

"But you shall not breathe when you are dust"

No recantation took place and the

Tribesmen, to the last, were pounded into nothingness.

Later that day the rains set in, and they did not cease for many a month. When they finally subsided, the dust of the Tribesmen was found to have been washed over the land of the Creators.

It could even be found drifting in the air and hiding in all the corners every-abode. Nowhere could one go to escape the dust; it covered everything and everyone.

    And what is more, it breathed.

Whatever is Not Forbidden

▼

In that age when Civilization again rose from the dust little remained of people or things. No this is not the place to tell that tale -- details can be found in the textbooks of the General History--but let us suffice to say that the new kings acted in a manner beholden of their natural lot when they prescribed the *Law of the X Nots* and *Transcript of the XII Don'ts* to hold the populace in their sway. Then this proved insufficient to further their nefarious aims *of* keeping (1) the dancers from dancing and {2) the dreamers from dreaming what came to be called The Great Dictum was finally invoked:

WHATEVER IS NOT FORBIDDEN IS RERQUIRED

11.9 (24:8) #384

Selected Bibliography

Some 400 works of Paul JJ Payack have appeared in scores of collections, anthologies and reviews the world over. This is a representative sampling.

"Acropolis Apocalypse," collage, New Letters

"Agglutination of Speech," metafiction, Outpost

"Anatomical Plates," selections from the collage biography, New Letters

"Atomic Number 7 (a Short Life)," metafiction, Wetlands

"At the Burial of a Dead Idea," metafiction, Cambridge Phone-a-Poem

"ATTN:" metafiction, Stone Soup

"Babel," metafiction, Centaur

"A Bed of Moss," metafiction, Centaur

"Between Chaos and the Commonplace," metafiction, Creative Computing

"The Black Hole," metafiction, Star-web Papers

"The Black Lists," collection, Chthon Press

"The Borning of Empire," Star-web Papers

"Ablata At Alba," metafiction, Circle

"Chronophobia," metafiction and sky art, Boston First Night

"Chthon," metafiction, Ripples

"A City Besieged by Dreams," metafiction, Huck Finn Review

"Collapsing Into Sand," metafiction, Wetlands

Conversation With the WordMan 106

"Commonplace Remark," metafiction, Bark

"Computer Misprint," prose poem, The Paris Review

"Conditioned Reflex," prose poem, The Paris Review

"Conversation with The WordMan (An Interview With the Inventor of Words)," yourDictionary.com

"Crack in the Cosmic Egg," prose poem, The Paris Review

"The Cracks of Silence," metafiction, Omni

"Dancing in Starbeams," metafiction, Star-web Papers

"Daring the Fearful Things," metafiction, Huck Finn Review

"A Day in the Life of the Philosopher," metafiction, Chunga Review

"Day of Judgment," collage, New Letters

"A Deathless Gift (to the Death-bound)," metafiction, Some Poetry

"The Death of the Creature of Light," metafiction, Zahir

"Debate Over the Existence of the Mind," polyplay, Outpost

"The Dénouement (or the Dark Cloud)," metafiction Third Eye

"Destroy All Dreamers (The Gadget)," metafiction, Huck Finn Review

"The Dim Lamp," metafiction, Phantasm

"Dispatch from the Front Lines," collage essay, iUniverse

"Frontispiece," collage

"Architectural Elements," collage

"Betwixt Sticks," collage

"Doric Column," collage

"Inflexion Point," collage

"Lightning Strike," collage

Selected Bibliography 107

"Purple Sage," collage

"Sky-fallen," collage

"Sounding Horns," collage

"Stalactites," collage

"Star-flower," collage

"Vapour Trails," collage

"Nightwings," collage

"The Final Toll," collage

"Dissonance, History, and Counterpoint," metafiction, Velvet Wings

"The Divine Comedy: A Post-Modern Commentary," selections from the collage narrative, New Letters

"Doe or Zho," metafiction, New Letters

"Dream (Stone-clouds, No. 2)," metafiction, Phantasm

"The Dream-child," metafiction, Quoin

"Dream/Line 2," metafiction, Sunflower Gazette

"The Dustbin of History," essay, New Infinity Review

"Dynamic Symmetry," metafiction, Phantasm

"Elektron," metafiction, Star-web Papers

"The Eleventh Commandment," metafiction, Walloon

"E=MC2," metafiction, Star-web Papers

"The End of Empire: The Paris Plates," selections in New Letters

"The End of the Dark Ages," metafiction, Third Eye

"The Eradication of Radicals," metafiction, Modus Operandi

"Esteemed Formalities," metafiction, Fish

Conversation With The WordMan

Conversation With the WordMan: An Interview With the Inventor of Words

The Alphabet: The Eye, the Needle and the Ox

The Tangles of Time: A Brief History of Chess

The Careless Steps of a Gull: A Note on Marginalia

Cornerstones: Events That Stand as Demarcations in Time

Daring the Fearful Thing: Adapted from Euripides

A Day in the Life of the Philosopher: (A Life Inextricably Entwined in Words)

A Dead Man's Tongue: Anubis Weighs In

Doe or Zho? A Princely Predicament

Dream Sequence No. 2: Aristotle (384–322 B.C) .

Dream Sequence No. 6: Johann Sebastian Bach (A.D. 1685–1750)

The Dustbin of History: How the Infinity Symbol Came Into Existence

The Eradication of Radicals: Acting Upon an Erroneous Definition

Eve of the Ides: A Notable Happenstance on the Ides of March

The Final Farewell: The Official End of the 20th Century

Footnotes: An Addendum to the Battle of Marathon

Forbidden Fields: Shields Green's Only Known Words

Found on a Misplaced Microdot: Extricating the Tune

The Geomancers: The Intersection of Philosophy and Engineering

The Great Chain of Being: The Pentateuch Translated Into Greek

Ideas Dissolved: A Note on Ideograms

In Tapestry and Reality: A Note Upon the Unicorn

The Knower and the No'er: Her Role in Your Creative Development

The Lament: The Last Words of the Last Speaker of the Proto-Indo-European Language

The Law of the Persistence of Entities: The Difficulty in Ending Any Creative Endeavour

Lowell, Mon Amour: The City as Dream Factory

Many and Fickle: The Whims of History

Monoliths of Stone: The Historical Position of the Onion

The More is More Principle: Toward A Radical New Vision for Management by Paiacus

Mythomania: A Certified Case of Dementia Mythos

Not to be Dwarfed: On Beginning New Orders .

The Number of Words in the English Language: The WordMan's

Of All Yet for None: The Sphinx

On the Authority of Tradition: The Day of Frigga

A Short Digression Upon Meilgaard: Never to Know, Always to Fear

Star-splitter: The Orion Nebula

Steppingstone to the Stars: Or How the Zero Was Discovered

'Solutions Selling': Sales Lingo (The Breaking Fast Experience)

The Ten UnCommandments of CorporateSpeak™: Corpbonics™

The Universal History of Mankind: The Last Five Lines

Unsolicited Advice To Young Writers: Upon Finding One's Voice

The Versificators: An Excerpt from Worlds to Shatter, Shattered Worlds concerning the Biblioclasts

The Wall Builders: Without Exception

Why The Universal Library Was Never Discovered: A Web of Darkness

Zanichelli's Tale: The Dream Table

"Excerpt," metafiction, Phantasm

"Eyewitness Account," metafiction, Some Poetry

"The Face of God," metafiction, Ripples

"The Face of His Father," metafiction, New Letters

"Factotum," metafiction, Truly Fine Press

"The Final Farewell: The Official End to the Twentieth Century," essay, yourDictionary.com

"Follow the Wind," metafiction, New York Culture Review

"Found on a Misplaced Microdot," prose poem, The Paris Review

"Gare du Fear," collage, New Letters

"The Great Chain of Being," metafiction, Zahir

"High Sky, Low Tide," collage, New Letters

"The History of Science in Five Easy Lessons," metafiction, Velvet Wings

"The Hostage," metafiction, Veins

"I am God," metafiction, Mirror Northwest

"The Idea Mine, or a Brief Note on Metafiction", iUniverse

"Indirect, Dubious, & Unintelligible," metafiction, Ruhtra

"The Ineffable Pathway," metafiction, Yellow Brick Road

"Information Overload," metafiction, The Diversifier

"Intelligence Quotient," metafiction, Zone

"Just Another Form of Nothingness," metafiction, Lazy Fair

"Kopernik," metafiction, Lynx

Selected Bibliography 109

"The Lament (The Last Words of the Last Speaker of the Proto-Indo-European

Language)," metafiction, yourDictionary.com

"The Land God Forgot," metafiction, Cambridge Phone-a-Poem

"The Last to Quarrel," metafiction, Star-web Papers

"Legend of the Shaman," Windows in the Stone anthology, metafiction portfolio, Free Press

"Life of the Saint," prose poem, The Paris Review

"A Little Known Fact II," metafiction, Image

"A Little Known Fact III," metafiction, Image

"A Little Known Fact IV," metafiction, New Letters

"Memory, Forgetfulness & Being," prose poem, The Paris Review

"Microtales," collection, Quark Press

"The Midget's Tale," metafiction, Arete

"Monoliths of Stone," metafiction, Some Poetry

"Mortality Tales," collection, Chthon Press

"The Motto of the Empire," metafiction, Star-web Papers

"Mourning Glory," collage, New Letters

"The Murmur of Lazy Bees," metafiction, Star-web Papers

"Music of the Spheres," prose poem, The Paris Review

"Mutually Intelligible Response," polyplay, InCider

"Mythomania," collection, New York Culture Review Press

"Introduction," essay by Sylvia Leah Berkman

"Conditioned Reflex," metafiction

Conversation With the Word Man

"Music of the Spheres," metafiction

"Daring the Fearful Thing," metafiction

"The Alphabet," metafiction

"Computer Misprint," metafiction

"Found on a Misplaced Microdot," metafiction

"Between Chaos and the Commonplace," metafiction

Puffballs," metafiction

"Strange Waters," metafiction

"As Told by a Broken Tongue…," metafiction

"To Drop a Feather," metafiction

"The Most Staggering Event In the History of the Planet," metafiction

"Star-fallen," metafiction

"The Dream-child," metafiction

"Mythomania," metafiction

"Memory, Forgetfulness & Being," metafiction

"Memory, History & Perception," metafiction

"Life of the Saint," metafiction

"The Sands Below," metafiction

"A Crack in the Cosmic Egg," metafiction

"A Mythopoeic Thought," metafiction, New Earth Review

"The Naming of America," metafiction, Star-web Papers

"Ne Plus Ultra," metafiction, (Russian and English language editions), Gnosis Anthology

"New Wisdom," metafiction, New Letters

"Noble Savage," metafiction, Star-web Papers

"The Number of Words in the English Language (The WordMan's Perspective)," essay, yourDictionary.com

"Obde," metafiction, Fish

"On Bagging the Four Winds," metafiction, Modus Operandi

"On the Glory of his Nostrils (or the Idiot Savant)," metafiction, Fish

"On the Nature of Being," metafiction, Insight

"On the Nature of History," metafiction, New Letters

"Passing Comment," metafiction, Phantasm

"The Perspective Series," selections from the collage narrative, Boulevard

"Picturing Infinity," collage, Asimov's Science Fiction

"A Plague of Darkness," essay, iUniverse

"Acropolis Apocalypse," collage

"Forward March the Legions," collage

"Windchild," collage

"Afternoon Tea," collage

"Babylon, at Last!" collage

"Alas, Babylon!" collage

"Gare du Fear," collage

"Manifest Destiny," collage

"The Reading Circle," collage

"Sail Trimmer No. 1," collage

"Sail Trimmer No. 2," collage

"Sky Skimmer," collage

"Spilt Milk," collage

'…by a thread,' collage

Conversation With the WordMan

"Stately Slumber (Sleeping)," collage

"Therein Lies the Way," collage

"Sanctuary," collage

"Trestle Thistle," collage

"All is Forgiven," collage

"Recessional," collage

"Buffalo Stand, Bison Standing," collage

"Sky Skimming," collage

"Inundulations," collage

"Pushover (under)," collage

"Dainty Dollie," collage

"Vantage Point," collage

"Luminaria," collage

"Lingering Lad," collage

"Deflation," collage

"Station Slumber," collage

"Abiding Angel," collage

"Plain Speakin'," metafiction, Minotaur

"Polyethylene Wind," metafiction, Phantasm

"Puffballs (or the Mycologist)," metafiction, Quoin

"Quantum Silence," metafiction, Buffalo Gnats

"REMEMBER:: metafiction and sky art, Out-of-Town News (Harvard Square)

"A Ripple in Entropy," collection, Chthon Press

"Said the Man Who Built the Bomb (on the Day After the World Was

Destroyed)," metafiction, Chunga Review

"Santa and the Ho-Ho-Ho Zone by the Brothers Payack," Christmas tale and collages, Quark Press

"Shortest Tomes," collection, Chthon Press

"A Sleepless Night," metafiction, Aspect

"Spilt Milk," collage, New Letters

"Star-fallen," metafiction, Riverbottom

"Star-splitter," metafiction, New Letters

"The Star-Tales Cycle," collections, Samisdat Press

"Solstice I"

"Solstice II"

"Solstice III"

"The Steppingstone to the Stars, or How the Zero was Discovered," metafiction, yourDictionary.com

"Stonecloud," metafiction, St. George Review

"The Story of Ulc," metafiction, Bark

"Subsidiarity," metafiction, Nitty-Gritty

"The Tangles of Time (a Short History of Chess)," essay, yourDictionary.com

"Telling Remark," metafiction, Gargoyle

"Theory, Plenitude & Form," metafiction, Benzene

"The Tome," metafiction, Star-web Papers

"Tribal Memory," metafiction, Bark

"Triumph of the Will," metafiction, Fish

"Twist of Fate Number 3," metafiction, Inky Trails

Conversation With The WordMan 114

"The Unexpected Twist Series," collection, Quark Press

"Unexpected Twist Number 3 (Weak Imagery)," metafiction, Nitty-Gritty

"Unexpected Twist (Mutual Exclusion)," metafiction, St. George Review

"The Universal History of Mankind," metafiction, Lynx

"The Universe Makers," metafiction, Copper Toadstool

"The Wall of Wonder," collage, Asimov's Science Fiction

"The Ways of Grace Forsaken," metafiction, Velvet Wings

"What Manner of Thing?" metafiction, Modus Operandi

"What Might Have Been," metafiction, Fish

"What the Seers of the Past Are Able to Tell Us About the Present," metafiction, Samizdat

"Where the Stars Go to Die," metafiction, Truly Fine Press

"The Whisperer's Whisper," metafiction, New Earth Review

"White Night," metafiction, Cambridge Phone-a-Poem

"Windblown," metafiction, Bark

"The Wind Turbine Studies", collage essay, iUniverse

"The Wind Turbine Studies," title collage

"Return of the Gods," collage

"Wind Turbine Study No. 1 (Wind Child)," collage

"Wind Turbine Study No. 2," collage

"Fleur du Wind," collage

"Inverted Torso," collage

"Candlewick," collage

"Windflower," collage

Selected Bibliography 115

"Reveries," collage

"Stolen Kiss," collage

"Buffalo Skin," collage

"Ahoy!," collage

"Mother Anterior," collage

"Windflowering," collage

"Ephemera," collage

"Rolling Thunder," collage

"Artillery Advancing," collage

"Boleros," collage

"Tymphonic Tambours," collage

"Measure Twice," collage

"Windstrings," collage

"Wistful Memory," metafiction, Bark

"The Worm," metafiction, Yellow Brick Road

"Yankee Clipper at River Styx Station," collage, New Letters

"Yankee Ingenuity," metafiction, Yellow Brick Road

"The Ylianic Wars," reference table, Gargoyle

About

Paul JJ Payack

▼

"The brief, almost bald, summation of crucial experience that attains its power through its stark reductiveness".

— Sylvia Leah Berkman, from the
   Introduction to *Mythomania*

Paul JJ Payack has authored hundreds of what *The Paris Review* called 'prose poems,' *The Kansas City Star*, 'polyphonic prose,' and *Contemporary Authors*, 'metafiction'. Payack's work has appeared in hundreds of journals, anthologies, and collections including *The Paris Review*, *New Letters*, and *Boulevard*. Payack's oeuvre currently consists of some 1600 creative works.

His published works include some twenty books including *A Million Words and Counting (How Global English is re-writing the World)*, *The Dream Cycle* (Selected Tales on Dreams and Dreaming), *Children of the Mind* (Hidden History Edition) written with Francois Larosa, *The Angel's Song (How the Children Saved the World from the Pandemic),* written with Peter Payack, *Santa and the Ho-Ho-Ho Zone* (2021 Edition), written with Peter Payack, *The Idea Mine, A Brief Note on Metafiction* (Autobiography), *Children of the Mind* (Steampunk Edition), *Conversation with the WordMan and Other Words on Words, A Plague of Darkness, or The Unseen and the Unseeable,*(on the plight of children in contemporary society), *Worlds to Shatter, Shattered Worlds,(a play)*, *Mythomania* (with an Introduction by Sylvia .L Berkman), *The Black Lists of Melanchthon, A Ripple in Entropy* (written while a student at Harvard), among a number of others.

Payack has spent some thirty years as a marketing executive in the High-Tech arena, most recently in Silicon Valley. In addition, he is founder, president (and The WordMan) of both yourDictionary.com, and the Global Language Monitor, the Global English source of record.

As a media commentator, Payack provides incisive analysis of words and language for leading media outlets the world over, such as: *the BBC; The Wall Street Journal; The New York Times; CNN; The Times of London; The Australian Broadcasting Corporation;* and *National Public Radio* and Public Radio International (NPR/ PRI); and participated in the White House High Tech CEO Forum, just weeks before the events of September 11th, 2001.

Payack attended Bucknell where he studied psychology and philosophy and was graduated from Harvard University where he studied comparative literature, fine arts, and a variety of dead languages.

He currently resides in Austin, Texas with his wife, Millie, and family.

Index

'non-parallel' or 'oblique' 116
"Give Us Back Our Minds" 118
"We Want Dreams" 118
a better-informed God 63
a city besieged by dreams. 107
A LESSER GOD 119
a professional dreamer by trade 70
Akhenaton 96
an Automaton 61
an oblique artifact 116
an outbreak of peace 107
ancient dreams 42
ancient dreams to be modern nightmares ... 99
anti-mirage drugs 92
Applied Metaphysics 60
Aristotle 44
Ashes of my Dreams 54
assorted idiocies 25
Austin, Texas 143
Bibliography 127
born today and dead yesterday 19
borning and dying of empires 49
Boulevard 142
box of dreams 43
branding BELIEVER and HEATHEN into the foreheads 76
Bucknell 143
Catechism 18
Center for the Struggle Against Ideological Deviation 40
Citadel of the Infidel 46
City as Dream Factory 131
City of Spires 66
complex matrices of amino acids,119, *See* Dreams
Consciousness 47
Crown of Immortality 43, 88
crucial experience 141
crystallization of the unconscious ' 44
cuneiform 96
Deep Thinker 25
dementia mythos 58
Department of the Struggle Against Ideological Deviation: 85
DHGHOMYO 121
Doomsday Philosophers 56
Dream-child 120
Dreamer of 'Air Castles' 17
Dreamers and Thinkers 19
dreamers are considered superfluous 25
DREAMIUM 74
dream-latchers 118
dreams as a dihedral angle 121
dreams of dead geniuses 57
Dream-table 74
dream-vision 80
dust of departed dragons 98
dustboard 96
duty of the Technocrats 55
Duty of the Technocrats 55
Eight Things Elicited by the Arrival of Comets 31
ENDLESS WAR 115
Ethleback 54
Euclid 57
Euripides 70
Evil-mongers 30, 66
Eye of God 97
faded memories 42
false epistemology 44
false hopes 42
fields sown with false hopes 42
finding Truth in a well 17
fools' paradise 56
forgotten old truths 16
Glass Mountains 98
Godh
  not to be confused with God 77
graveyard of faded memories 42
Great Dictum 126
Gwalstoe 58
Hammurabi 96
Handbook of Ritual 29
Harvard 22
Harvard University 143
hissing of a serpent 33
hollowed-out earth 99
home for lost dreams 42
'In Distrust of Memory' 25
Innate knowledge 123
interchangeability of all human thought' ... 93
Inventor of Words 130

Iphigenia in Aulis .... See Euripides	peasants stormed the computers. 9
Jaffa 78	phase transitions 5
jot and a tittle	Polymath 11
the distinction between 80	polyphonic prose 14
Keeper of the Imperial Archives 43, 88	pre-Socratic Greeks 5
Knower and the No'er 131	Procurator 1
Land of YNCE 20	prognosis death 3
Land of YNCE (inch) 37	prophet by trade 1
Land of Zelotyp 79	Recurring dreams 3
Last of the Last 44	register his mind as a weapon. 5
Law of the X Nots 126	residue of the Dreams 2
lost dreams 42	Right to Dream 4
lured by the Dreams 102	Ruling Lord of Thebes 9
magnetic bottles 55	Secret Police 87, 9
Magnetic Monopole 73, 120	'Secret Police 5
MANNA, AMBROSIA and the MANDU 26	setting the controls for TRUTH 5
Mathano 22	seven auditory impressions 6
Mathematico 22	seven breathings of a baby 6
Mathematico; 22	seven drops of blood 6
medieval scriptorium 62	seven extirpated eyes 6
Melampos 17	seven intonations of the unconscious 6
Mesopotamia 96	seven minds of the children 6
metafiction 142	seven mirrors of the other 6
Metafiction	seven swallowings of the sky 6
On the Nature of 94	seven wailings of the wind. 6
middle-level Celestial official 62	shuffling of feet 3
Mildtryth 118	Slayer of Dreams .... See
Millie 143	societal amnesia 11
multi-dimensional non-dimension 55	sound of a shepherd's pipe 3
Myllye 70	splash of water 3
Mysteries of Fate 47	standardization of ideas 9
MYTHIUM 75	stark reductiveness 14
Naxos 46	strangeness of every quark 4
'neural* model of reality 76	Sumerians 9
New Letters 142	Sylvia Leah Berkman 14
New Vision 45	Table of Contents ....
Nha 93	textbooks of the General History 12
Nineveh, ... 77	Thaab, the Dream-slayer 5
Noers-of-Nothingness 124	The Bottom Line, ... 3
Note on Marginalia 130	The Chronicles 11
oblique artifact 116	the Citadel 10
Oblique obfuscations 122	the COSMOLOGIA 10
Official Searcher of Hearts 43	The Dream-drive 11
outbreak of peace 66	the Dreams 9
outline of the Cosmos 48	The Dreams
over the Endless Mountains 70	Mined the last of 9
Paiacus 131	the Evil Endless Realm 2
Paris Review 141	the Eye of God 9
Paul JJ Payack 141	the Facilitators 6
PAXIUM 74	*The Future Belongs to those Who Dare.* 2

the infinitude of Time	48
the nebulized	116
The Other	121
The Paris Review	*142*
the Procurator	19
The Secret of Time	123
The Society	57
The Tales'	118
the teeming is of the mind	36
the tomb of the muses	123
THE UNPERSON	18
the unreality principle	122
The Usurper	54
The wizard	32
The WordMan	142
thing both existent and non-existent	121
thing existing neither io quantity nor spatial continuity	121
THINKERS	45
thought-catchers	118
thousand Black Butterflies	66
Thousand Infinities,	105
to erase History	93
TO SLEEP IS TO LET THEM DIE	57
totality of existence	48
Transcript of the XII Don'ts	126
TRUTH	32, 40
TRUTHIUM	74
ULČ	102
unborn tomorrow and dead yesterday	104
Unspeakings of the Unperson	104
VERITAS	35
very ancient dreams	16
victory of the Tower	70
WE US THEY THEM	104
what is a dream?	121
whistling of an arrow	32
Widener library	21
Wyclif	62
Xoa	70
Yellow Icarus	98
yourDictionary.com	138
Zanichelli	74
Zencle	38
Zero	96
Zyblya	28

The Dream Cycle

Selected Metafictions on Dreams and Dreaming

Paul JJ Payack

Chthon Press/Assembly Line Studio.

Designed, Published and Printed in the United States of America

Copyright ©2022 by Paul JJ Payack

First Edition

All Rights Reserved

For more information and interviews, call 1.737.215.7750 or email pjjp@post.harvard.edu

Chthon Press, Austin, Texas, 2022

Made in the USA
Coppell, TX
06 July 2024